super Emma

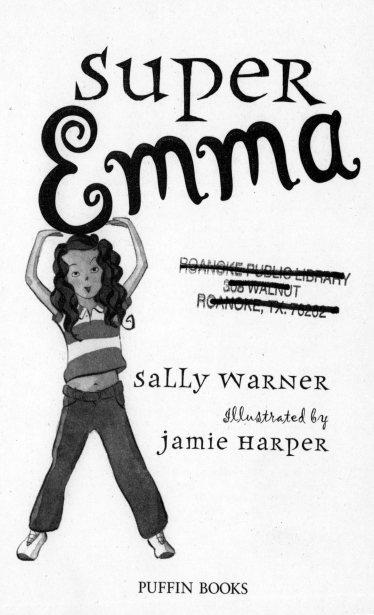

saLLy WARNER

Illustrated by
jamie HARper

PUFFIN BOOKS

PUFFIN BOOKS

Published by the Penguin Group

Penguin Young Readers Group, 345 Hudson Street, New York, New York 10014, U.S.A.

Penguin Group (Canada), 90 Eglinton Avenue East, Suite 700,
Toronto, Ontario, Canada M4P 2Y3 (a division of Pearson Penguin Canada Inc.)

Penguin Books Ltd, 80 Strand, London WC2R 0RL, England

Penguin Ireland, 25 St Stephen's Green, Dublin 2, Ireland
(a division of Penguin Books Ltd)

Penguin Group (Australia), 250 Camberwell Road, Camberwell, Victoria 3124, Australia
(a division of Pearson Australia Group Pty Ltd)

Penguin Books India Pvt Ltd, 11 Community Centre,
Panchsheel Park, New Delhi - 110 017, India

Penguin Group (NZ), 67 Apollo Drive, Rosedale, North Shore 0632, New Zealand
(a division of Pearson New Zealand Ltd)

Penguin Books (South Africa) (Pty) Ltd, 24 Sturdee Avenue,
Rosebank, Johannesburg 2196, South Africa

Registered Offices: Penguin Books Ltd, 80 Strand, London WC2R 0RL, England

First published in the United States of America by Viking,
a division of Penguin Young Readers Group, 2006

Published by Puffin Books, a division of Penguin Young Readers Group, 2008

1 3 5 7 9 10 8 6 4 2

Text copyright © Sally Warner, 2006
Illustrations copyright © Jamie Harper, 2006
All rights reserved

LIBRARY OF CONGRESS CATALOGING-IN-PUBLICATION DATA IS AVAILABLE
ISBN: 0-670-06140-9 (hc)

Puffin Books ISBN 978-0-14-241088-2

Printed in the United States of America
Set in Bitstream Carmina
Book design by Nancy Brennan

For Joe Martin, my main (super) man
in Madison, Wisconsin—S.W.

x x x

For Gonna—J.H.

CONTEN

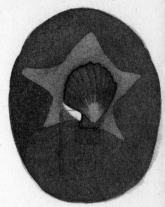

ts

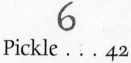

1

For No Reason

"Let me see that, stupid," Jared Matthews says to EllRay Jakes. "Give it here." If Jared were a lion, he would be growling right now. His twirly brown hair even looks a little like a lion's mane, if you squint your eyes.

But that's not fair to lions, one of my favorite animals.

"My name's not 'Stupid,' *stupid*, it's EllRay," EllRay tells him, trying to be brave. But he hands over the plastic figure he was playing with to Jared, who grabs it and starts twisting the movable arms back and forth.

Lions can run the length of a football field in six seconds.

"Don't break the wings," EllRay says in a loud and nervous voice.

I have said it before: EllRay is small in size but large in noise. He is the first littlest kid in the third grade, and I am the second littlest. Also, I am the second shyest, after Fiona.

I don't like to hear EllRay sound scared. I think he's pretty cool, but that's a secret.

"I'll break the wings if I want to, *Lancelot*," Jared says.

Lancelot!

See, I think the trouble started this morning when we had this substitute teacher, Mrs. Matheson. She's short and wide, and she was wearing an orange dress that made her look like a big chunk of supermarket cheese.

Well, she still is. Wearing the dress, I mean.

Anyway, she called EllRay

by his real name. She said, "Lancelot Raymond Jakes?" while she was taking roll. And I guess EllRay's name was supposed to be a secret, because he never said it out loud before.

A lot of kids laughed when the substitute called his name, but Jared Matthews laughed the loudest: *"Haw, haw, haw."* He is the biggest kid in our third-grade class, and he is not very nice.

"My name is EllRay," EllRay shouted politely to Mrs. Matheson, but it was too late—the damage was done. Now, everyone in class knows that EllRay is probably short for L-period-Ray, which is probably short for Lancelot Raymond.

Some people's mothers and fathers should

be more careful when they name a baby, that's what I think.

Jared pinches the toy's purple wing, which is webbed like a bat's. It is as if he is holding a tea-cup he is about to smash on the ground. He looks at EllRay, just daring him to say something. And Jared is smiling a little. "I think wings look dumb on action figures," he says to EllRay.

EllRay's eyes get big. He looks scared—or at least very wide awake.

Wide awake is a good way to look in our class, especially after lunch on a warm California day. It is very easy to fall asleep then, even if you pretend that you are only reading up close. And doing that just makes me sleepier than ever, which is why we get a recess like this in the afternoon—to run around and breathe some fresh air, in other words.

Oh, that reminds me! This boy Corey Robinson, who sits next to me, really fell all the way asleep in class last week. He even drooled on his book, which is official school property. I felt sorry for him, but it was kind of funny.

It was *especially* funny when Ms. Sanchez, who is our regular teacher, glided up behind him and pinched him on his hot red ear. Even though it was a gentle pinch, Corey squawked like a stepped-on cat, and he rose straight up into the air as if his chair was a giant slingshot that had decided to see how far Corey and his floppy green hair would go.

The answer was—pretty far!

In case you are wondering, Corey is not an outer-space alien, even though he has green hair. He is training to be a swimming champion, which is another classroom secret, but he told me about it once. Anyway, Corey swims a lot, and sometimes the chlorine in the pool turns his whitey-blond hair green.

He always smells very clean, though, and I think he is going to be in the Olympics someday.

You have to start early for that.

During EllRay's fight with Jared, Corey is standing behind EllRay, and a bunch of girls stand beside Corey, including me. Corey is moving from foot to foot as if the Oak Glen Primary School playground is as hot as a barbecue grill. He is glaring at large, mean Jared, but he doesn't actually say anything.

Corey and EllRay are friends. Well, those two guys are friends with Jared, too, usually. The weird part about this fight, and about most fights between boys, I have noticed, is that it was probably for no reason. That's why lots of things happen at this school.

"Give it back," EllRay yells, holding out his hand. Next to me, my new friend Annie Pat makes a worried noise in the back of her throat. I try to touch her arm to calm her down, but I can't stop looking at EllRay and Jared. I'm afraid I'll fall over or something if I try to do too many things at once.

My stomach is starting to feel all jangly, as

though the tuna in the sandwich I ate for lunch has started swimming around in there. Digesting my lunch might be trying to do one too many things, it suddenly occurs to me.

I hope I'm wrong about that, because barfing at school is the second worst thing that can happen to a kid.

"*Make* me give it back," Jared says calmly, as if nothing bad is happening. As if this is just an ordinary day.

EllRay takes a step forward. "I *will* make you give it back," he says in a shaky voice. "I'll—I'll—"

"You'll what?" Jared asks, sneering. "You'll tell the teacher on me?" He holds the figure tighter, smiles, and starts to bend the wing.

Everybody's breath gets sucked in at once. It sounds as though the wind is blowing by.

"No-o-o-o!" EllRay howls.

"Oh, oh," Heather echoes. That's her favorite expression.

Suddenly, from out of nowhere, someone

jumps out of the crowd and grabs the toy—right out of Jared Matthews's hand. "Quit it, you big bully," that person yells.

Hey, it's me! Emma McGraw!

x 2 x

a HERO

I must be the most surprised person in the world right now, because I am not exactly brave. I like peace and quiet too much for that.

But no, Jared is even more surprised than I am. He staggers back, and his jaw hangs open like a panting lizard's on a very hot day. He stares down at his hand as though he can't really believe it is empty.

Lizards smell with their tongues.

I shove the toy in EllRay's direction.

"She saved EllRay," someone whispers. "Emma saved EllRay—from Jared!"

"I only saved his toy," I try to say, but the

words get stuck in my throat when I see EllRay's face.

He doesn't look grateful, not one little bit.

"Ha-ha on Jared," one of the kids calls out.

"*Rah-h-h-h*," Jared roars, and he starts chasing that kid across the playground. He doesn't even look at me as he whizzes by.

"Emma, you're a hero," Annie Pat says to me, and she sounds awed. The afternoon sun shining behind her makes her curly red pigtails look as though they are on fire.

I clear my throat and sneak another look at EllRay Jakes. He is just standing there, and the action figure is drooping in his hand. "I'm not a hero," I say. "I only—"

"You only ruined everything," EllRay says. "Thanks a lot, *Emma*."

The way he says "Thanks," though, you can tell he doesn't mean it. He is mad at me, all right. But why?

EllRay and I stand very still for a second, staring at each other.

When the bell rings, it is as if it breaks a magic spell. The two of us can move again.

I never thought I would be so glad to get back to class, especially when we have a substitute teacher. Because when we have a substitute, the bad kids act up, and the good kids act nervous.

And if you're a good kid, which I usually am, what's so fun about that?

x 3 x

fOR NO REASON!

I am an only child, and that is not such a wonderful thing when you have an important question to ask an older brother or sister. A question such as this: *"Why is EllRay Jakes so mad at me?"*

My mom says that I can ask her anything, but sometimes I don't want to, because she gets worried when things aren't going perfectly right for me. So I keep pretty quiet most of the time.

But I have to ask her this one question. "Mom? Ow."

"Hold still, Emma," Mom says, holding on to a wet tangled hunk of my hair, which is long and brown. It smells like a mixture of apples and roses after I wash it. Mom is trying to work the comb through my hair.

"Ow," I remind her.

"This doesn't hurt," Mom informs me. "See," she says, "I'm holding it." Mom claims that if you pinch hair, you can comb the ends without it hurting. Luckily, hair doesn't feel pinches.

"Yes, but it might *start* hurting," I remind her. "Mom?" I try again.

"I'm still here," my mom says, moving her hands to another part of my head.

"Ow. Um, guess what happened during afternoon recess today?"

My mom stops combing. "What?" she asks. She already sounds concerned.

See, that's the trouble about not talking very

much about school. When you *do* talk, your mother listens too hard. I shake my head a little to remind her about the combing. "Well," I begin, "these two boys were having a fight." I peek up at her.

Mom's eyes get big and shiny. "A fight? *What* two boys?"

"No, wait, that's not the important part," I tell her. "Ow."

"What *is* the important part?" Mom asks. She tries to shove one of her sleeves up without letting go of my hair. She wiggles her nose as if it itches.

I sigh. "Well, the important part is that I was the one who made them stop fighting," I say. I leave out the part about me upsetting the boy-girl ecology of my entire class.

Mom stops combing again and pulls back a little. She looks at me as if she is watching *The Emma Channel* with all her might. "Good for you, Emma," she says, smiling. "I'm proud of you, honey."

Brown bear cubs live with their mothers for up to three years.

"Well, don't be," I tell her gloomily, "because now some kids hate me."

Mom scowls. "What kids?" she asks. She can be like a mother bear who wants to bite anyone who bothers her cub. I've seen it before, on Animal Planet.

I'm her cub, and that's another reason I don't tell her stuff, sometimes.

"It was Jared and EllRay," I say. "Jared took EllRay's toy during recess and then called him a name."

"A bad name?" Mom asks.

I think for a second. "Kind of," I finally say. "But it was actually EllRay's own real name."

Mom tilts her head. "Which *is*?" she asks, obviously expecting me to tell her EllRay's real name.

"Lancelot Raymond," I whisper. "We had a substitute, and she gave it away."

Now Mom shakes her head and smiles. "Poor EllRay," she says. "But how did *you* get involved, Emma? I just can't picture it."

"Me either," I admit, "but—I guess I jumped right in the middle of the fight and rescued EllRay's toy, then I gave it to him. He was scared of Jared, and I hated seeing that."

My mom scoops me into a hug and ruffles my wet hair. "I'm proud of you," she says again, whispering the words into my ear. It tickles.

"But I wasn't being brave," I tell her. "I didn't even think before I did it."

Mom gives me an extra squeeze. "Well," she says, "I can see how *Jared* might be a little bit irked, being shown up by a girl that way, but who else is angry with you?"

"EllRay is," I say, and I make a face to hide the way I feel—which is sad.

"Oh, dear."

"For no reason!"

"I have to say I'm not surprised," Mom says.

"But why?" I ask her.

Mom shrugs. "Maybe it's because he feels bad that he couldn't stick up for himself."

"But he probably would have," I say, "if I hadn't jumped in and done it first."

My mom stands up and stretches. "I think maybe you embarrassed EllRay a little, that's all. He'll get over it."

"But should I tell him I'm sorry?" I ask. I fiddle with my pajama top, which is all cold and wet around the neck, thanks to my hair.

"*Are* you sorry?"

"Yeah, I am. If I really embarrassed him, I mean. But I'm not sorry I made Jared look dumb in front of all those people. He's so mean to everyone!"

Mom plugs in the hair dryer. "Well, that's another problem for another day," she tells me.

Whnn-n-n. . . . The dryer starts its horrible noisy whine, which always hurts my ears, even though my mom doesn't believe it when I tell her that. Hair dryers are not good for peace and quiet, that's for sure. And they always smell funny, as if one little hair is burning somewhere inside them. "Ow," I say.

"Emma, for heaven's sake. I'm not even touching you yet."

"Oops—sorry," I mumble. "But tell me when you start, okay? So I can say 'Ow' again?"

And Mom just laughs.

⁂ 4 ⁂

Super Emma

Corey looks at me sideways the next morning when I take my seat. "You're late," he whispers. "I thought maybe you weren't coming to school today." A lock of hair flops onto his sunburned forehead.

"My mom's car wouldn't start, that's all," I tell him. Ms. Sanchez is back in class again, thank goodness, but she is busy at her desk looking at some papers. She hasn't taken roll yet. "Why wouldn't I come to school?" I ask Corey, keeping my voice low.

"*You* know," he says, blushing a little around his freckles.

And then Ms. Sanchez starts calling our names for attendance.

I can feel my own face getting hot as she says our names. *"You know"*? What's that supposed to mean?

But I can't ask Corey that out loud.

"EllRay Jakes," Ms. Sanchez calls out after

a few names, and a couple of kids wriggle and snicker at the sound of his name. You can hear someone whisper, *"Lancelot, Lancelot."* Ms. Sanchez pauses and looks up from her roll sheet.

The room holds still, because even though Ms. Sanchez is beautiful, she's also strict.

"Present," EllRay

says, his voice sounding loud and extra confident. He is wearing a big old football shirt today. EllRay likes to say "present" instead of "here" sometimes.

Ms. Sanchez gives him a little smile. Then she says, "Emma McGraw?"

"Here," I croak.

"Oh no, it's Super Emma," someone in the back row cries out. I think it's Stanley Washington. He hangs around Jared like one of those little fish that swims around a bigger sea creature, hoping for something good to eat.

Catfish have over 100,000 taste buds.

(Annie Pat wants to be a marine biologist who studies the beaked sea snake when she grows up, and I want to be a nature scientist, so we watch lots of videos and TV programs about wildlife. Nature is our favorite thing.)

When Stanley says "Super Emma" like that, everyone in class starts laughing. Everyone except

Ms. Sanchez, that is, and EllRay, and Jared, and Corey, and Annie Pat Masterson.

And me, Super Emma herself. Because "super" is something I do not want to be.

Ms. Sanchez stands up and claps her smooth hands together three times. We are lucky, because she is the prettiest teacher at Oak Glen Primary School by far. She is engaged to a man named Mr. Timberlake, but he's not the one on MTV. "Quiet down immediately," she calls out, scowling.

Uh-oh, she's *mad*. The noisy people in class quiet down—immediately—as ordered. The rest of us, who were quiet already, shrink down in our seats as though we are ice cream bars that are melting in the sun.

"Does anyone want to tell me just what . . . is . . . going . . . on . . . here?" Ms. Sanchez asks slowly.

No one does, of course.

"Mister Washington?" Ms. Sanchez says to Stanley.

We all turn around in our seats and stare at him. Stanley has never gotten so much attention in his whole life so far, I'll bet—and he hates it. Hah! It serves him right. He shakes his big head "no" so fast that his face looks blurry.

"Emma?" Ms. Sanchez says, turning to me.

"I—I don't know," I say, and I am telling the truth, because what *is* going on? Why did Stanley call me "Super Emma" in that making-fun way—when the only thing in the world that I was doing was sitting here trying to figure out how to tell EllRay at recess that I was sorry for embarrassing him yesterday?

"Then I'll continue," Ms. Sanchez tells us, zooming her sparkly brown eyes around the room one last time.

And so she does.

× × ×

Cynthia Harbison turns to me during morning recess. "You really messed up yesterday," she says. And then she grins. Next to her, Heather nods, looking wise—which is an optical illusion, believe me.

It is hot out today, even though it is almost Halloween. The third-grade girls are huddled in one shady patch of the playground, and the boys are gathered in another puddle of shade. Jared and EllRay are talking together as if nothing bad happened yesterday. It is as though someone has drawn a chalk line across the middle of the play-ground to keep the boys and the girls apart.

It's almost always like that around here.

I wish I didn't have to say anything back to Cynthia, but I do. "How did *I* mess up?" I ask, scuffing my sneaker on the bumpy black asphalt.

"You did a boy-thing," Cynthia informs me. Heather nods again, and now Fiona does, too—as if a nod is something that you can catch, like a cold.

But Annie Pat is not nodding. She is angry. "You guys all thought Emma was so brave yes-terday," she says, "and now you're being mean to her. That's not fair."

Cynthia shrugs and shakes the crumbs out of her empty plastic snack bag. Then she folds the bag up, as if she's really going to use it again. And I happen to know that Cynthia is not a good recycler. "That was yesterday," she says. "This is today."

"EllRay isn't glad that Super Emma saved his toy," Heather points out.

Annie Pat stomps her foot, and her red pigtails bounce. "Stop calling her Super Emma!"

"Yeah, quit it," I say, finding my voice again. It's a little squeaky. I don't sound very super, that's for sure.

Heather cringes, pretending to be afraid. "Oh, *please* don't hit me, Super Emma," she says. She peeks at Cynthia to see if she is laughing—which she is.

"You guys are just dumb," Annie Pat says. "Emma did a good thing yesterday."

"Emma did a *boy*-thing," Cynthia says, as if she is Ms. Sanchez correcting one of us kids.

"Being brave isn't just a boy-thing," Annie Pat says. She folds her arms across her chest.

"Yeah, you're right—it's a *stupid* thing," Heather zips back. She gives Cynthia another look, and Cynthia is the one to nod this time.

"It's a stupid thing to you, maybe," Annie Pat says. "Not to me."

Cynthia squints her eyes. "Well then, why don't you and Emma go over there and play with the boys, if you like them so much?" she says.

"We *don't* like them so much," I object, but nobody seems to hear me.

"Yeah," Fiona is saying. "Go play with Jared and EllRay and Stanley, if you like them so much." And Fiona is usually the shyest girl in class!

I can feel a tickle of sweat creep down my back.

"Come on, Emma," Annie Pat says, tugging at my sleeve. "We can tell when we're not wanted. Let's go."

I don't want to go.

I *want* to be wanted by the girls.

But I turn around and leave with Annie Pat anyway. Because what choice do we have? We have been banished.

x 5 x

fOR NO REASON?

EllRay comes up to me in the cloakroom right after the bell rings for lunch. I pretend that I am busy trying to find my lunch in my backpack, but I can see Jared and Stanley watching him from the doorway. EllRay looks nervous, but he straightens his big football shirt and says, "Mind your own business next time, stupid."

Stupid. That's what Jared called EllRay yesterday.

I feel like telling EllRay, *"Sure, I'll mind my own business—as soon as you stop acting like such a baby around Jared Matthews."* But I don't.

I don't apologize for embarrassing him yesterday, either—because I don't feel like it anymore. Who cares if EllRay was embarrassed?

"Did you hear me?" EllRay asks, after a quick look over his skinny shoulder tells him that Jared and Stanley are still watching us.

"Yeah, I heard you, *Lancelot*," I hear myself say. "And you can save your own doll, next time."

Wow, I didn't know I could be so mean! A couple of kids nearby whisper, excited.

EllRay blushes. "Huh. I'd rather be called

'Lancelot' than 'Super Emma' any day," he says, which doesn't make any sense at all. But EllRay *looks* as though it makes sense, or he tries to. "And anyway," he adds, "it's not a doll, it's an action figure."

"That's just stupid," I say, echoing the same word EllRay just used on me.

"You're the one who's stupid, stupid," EllRay zips back.

"No, you are. Why are you so scared of Jared, anyway?" I ask.

Uh-oh. Now, EllRay looks like he *really* hates me. But instead of answering my question, he just whirls around and stomps away.

"Well, *I'm* scared of Jared," Annie Pat whispers to me. I was so busy fighting that I didn't even see her standing there.

"Not me," I say, but it is a lie. Because who wouldn't be afraid of a kid who makes little kindergartners cry, telling them they can't use the drinking fountain—unless they hop on one leg first?

Or who wouldn't be afraid of a kid who got sent to the office for coloring the end of Fiona's long, light-brown braid with a purple felt-tip marker?

Or who wouldn't be afraid of

a kid who made a first-grader wet his pants because he wouldn't let him use the bathroom? And then Jared called him "Wetsy" for the rest of the week.

Or who wouldn't be afraid of a kid who makes you give him your dessert if it looks better than his? I heard he did that to Corey once in the second grade, when Corey brought a piece of birthday cake to school. With a yellow frosting rose on it.

It's not just that Jared (or Jar-Head, which is my secret name for him) is the biggest and strongest kid in the third grade, even though that is true. But I think he is a kid who likes to do mean things for no reason. It's as though Jared thinks that other kids are just there for him to have fun with. As if we're not real or something.

But *I'm* real, so that proves he's wrong.

"Let's go eat," Annie Pat says, nudging me with her freckled elbow.

"Where?" I ask her. Nobody will eat with us now, I guess, so we are running out of places.

"Under the pergola," Annie Pat says, as if she has been thinking about it all morning long.

The first-graders usually are the ones to eat in the striped shade of the pergola. It's almost like an invisible playpen, in my opinion.

"They're little. They won't bother us," Annie Pat says as if she is reading my mind.

I sigh. "Okay," I say. "Let's go."

X X X

I am munching my way through the last part of a spicy salami sandwich when someone taps on my shoulder with a hard, pointy finger. As I look around, I see a bunch of first-graders scatter the way birds do when a cat strolls by.

"Hey, dummy," Jared says to me. Stanley, EllRay, and Corey are standing behind him like a small flock of silly sheep. Corey looks as if he is about to faint. His face is so pale under his green hair that I bet I could count each freckle on it.

Well, one good thing—at least Jared's not

calling me "Super Emma." I try to swallow my bite of sandwich. Across from me, Annie Pat is goggling.

Ms. Sanchez does not like us to say "Hey," by the way. She says it is vulgar. She has very high hopes for us—including Jared, even.

Jared is scowling, probably because I have not said anything back to him. "You think you're so great, don't you?" he asks me. "Little Emma-Wemma, the perfect girl."

Stanley snickers when Jared calls me "Little Emma-Wemma."

"I don't think I'm so great," I say. I can hear my own heart beating, *wuh*, *wuh*, *wuh*.

"You do too think you're so great," Jared says, "calling EllRay 'Lancelot' and grabbing things that don't belong to you."

And all I can do is stare at Jared, because—because the subsitute was the one who called EllRay "Lancelot" first, and then Jared did. And *he's* the one who grabbed EllRay's toy, before I did. And here he is, picking on me for no reason!

What a coward.

"That's not fair," Annie Pat says, almost squeaking. I can't see her, because she's behind me now.

"Shut up," Jared says without even looking at her. "You're going to be sorry," he says to me. "You made me look stupid."

"Well, that's okay," I say fast, "because everyone already *knows* you're stupid."

What I really wanted to say, though, was that I *am* sorry. Not for making Jared look dumb, and not even for embarrassing EllRay. No, I'm sorry that I didn't have the measles this week, that's what I'm sorry about! Then I would have gotten to stay home, and none of this would have happened.

Jared takes a deep, deep breath and seems to swell up even larger than he is, which is plenty big already. But just as he is about to speak, a teacher who is one of the lunchtime monitors appears, his big face gleaming. "Is there a problem here?" he asks Jared.

The teacher is really saying, *"There had better not be."*

"No," Stanley Washington pipes up. "This girl was just bothering us," he says, pointing to me. "But that's all right," he adds in a forgiving way.

Hah!

Just then the bell rings, and it is like a game of musical chairs in reverse, because most of the kids under the pergola get up and run. "Throw your trash away," the playground teacher calls out, turning away.

But Jared's not going anywhere. "You're going to be sorry, Super Emma," he says again, leaning toward me and keeping his voice low. "I'm going to get even with you tomorrow at recess, when everyone on the playground is watching. Everyone!"

Pickle

"I think I'm getting a sore throat," I tell my mom while we are eating dinner.

"Oh, no," Mom says, putting down her fork. My mother works at home, so when I get sick it ruins everything for her. She reaches over and feels my forehead to see if I have a fever. She always frowns and looks up at the ceiling when she does this.

"I was a lot hotter before dinner," I tell her. I rub the front of my neck the way a person might do if she *really* had a sore throat. I cough a little. "I guess I'd better not go to school tomorrow," I say, looking weak and sad. I spear a big bite of meat loaf and dip it in a blob of ketchup.

Mom tilts her head and grins at me. "Well," she says, "you're sure wolfing down that meat loaf pretty fast for someone with such a bad sore throat."

Uh-oh. But I wish I *were* a wolf, except for the part where you have to spray your territory. (Look it up. I'm not explaining it any more than I already did.) Wolves are very clever, though. They would never get into this much trouble at school. "I'm just trying to keep up my strength,"

Wolves hold their tails high to show leadership.

I tell her, but I already know that she doesn't believe me about the sore throat.

"So what's going on at school tomorrow?" Mom asks. "Let me guess. A spelling test? A math quiz?"

"I *wish*," I say. I can feel my eyes start to get prickly, the way they do just before tears start to fall. My nose turns pink then, too.

"Emma," my mom says, looking serious

again, "what's the matter, honey? You look like you're about to cry."

I stare down at my mushed-up baked potato. "I—I *can't* go to school tomorrow," I tell my mom. "Because Jared's going to beat me up if I do."

Mom's fork drops with a clunk. "He actually *threatened* you?" she asks me.

Hot tears splash down my cheeks. "Yes," I tell her. "He said that he was going to get even with me in front of everybody on the playground, and that I would be sorry. I'm *already* sorry, only I won't tell Jared that. So that's it for me. Kiss me goodbye!"

"Oh, honey," Mom exclaims, and she scoots her chair back and holds out her arms, so I dive into her lap. She makes a noise that sounds like "*urf.*" And I can't help it—I cry for a little while, and she rubs my back, saying, "There, there."

Sometimes I feel like saying, *"Where, where?"* when she does that.

"I'm scared," I tell my mom. "Jared's so big and mean!"

"But Emma," Mom says, "I'm sure he would never really hit you. You've stood up to him before, right? You did it just yesterday, in fact."

"Mom, I *told* you! I wasn't thinking when I grabbed EllRay's toy away from him, so that doesn't count. See, that's the trouble," I tell her.

"What's the trouble?"

"Everyone thinks I was trying to be so brave," I say, sniffling. "They were even calling me Su-Su-*Super* Emma all day long."

Mom gives me a little hug. "Well, that's not such a bad nickname, is it? I think it's pretty cool, in fact."

"It was bad the way *they* said it," I tell her.

"And then even today, Annie Pat thought I was being brave again when Jared started picking on me and I called him a name. And I wasn't being brave, I was being mad—mad and scared. That's not the same thing as brave, is it? So it really doesn't count, either."

"But Emma . . ."

"I don't *want* to be brave," I interrupt. "I just want everyone to leave me alone!"

Mom ruffles my tangly hair. "Honey, 'brave' is only a word. It can mean a lot of different things. But did you apologize to EllRay the way we talked about—for embarrassing him yesterday?" she asks me.

"I never got a *cha-a-a-ance*," I wail. "He was too busy being mean to me! Oh, don't make me go to school tomorrow, okay? Have mercy!"

"Well, honey," my mom says in her most reasonable voice, "you're going to have to return to school sooner or later, so it might as well be tomorrow. Does Ms. Sanchez know any of this is going on?"

"She knows they're calling me 'Super Emma,' anyway," I say gloomily, wiping my face on my sleeve. "But she probably doesn't know why."

"Maybe I should go in and talk to her," Mom suggests. "Perhaps that would help."

"No, that would *hurt*," I tell her. "Ms. Sanchez can't follow Jared around for the rest of his life, can she?"

"Of course not," Mom says.

"Then sooner or later, he'll get me," I tell her.

"But Emma, if he threatened to beat you up, I—"

"He—he didn't exactly say he would beat me *up*," I admit. "He said he would get even with me. In front of all the kids. At recess tomorrow."

"Hmm," Mom says, thinking.

"You'll just make everything worse if you tell Ms. Sanchez," I tell her. "Promise you won't."

"But listen, Emma," Mom says, "you're really in a pickle here, and I think you need some help getting out of it."

Mom says "in a pickle" when she means that a person is in trouble. Or else she says "in a jam." She likes food talk, I guess.

"Well, maybe I could get out of the pickle if I stayed home tomorrow," I suggest, snuggling up. I am trying to remind her of our long history together. We go way back.

"That's no solution," Mom says, sighing.

"Then I'm going to be pickle-*relish*," I tell her. "That's all. But I'll go to school if you really want me to," I add. "I might as well get it over with."

It feels as though there is a rock in my stomach. But I climb out of her lap, sit down again in my own chair, stab another bite of meat loaf, dip it, and then chomp it as hard as I can.

Mom watches me and just shakes her head. "You're braver than you think you are, honey," she says.

Huh, I think, *that's easy for her to say.*

7

for No Reason

My mom pulls our car up under the big pepper tree in front of our school. She reaches over and twiddles with my hair. "Now remember, honey," she says, "if things look like they are getting out of control with Jared, I want you to tell Ms. Sanchez—at once. Do you promise me?"

"Okay," I say, crossing my fingers where she can't see them. I straighten them for a second to undo my seat belt, and then I grab my back-pack.

"I'll be home all day," Mom continues. "You call me if—if anything happens."

She means if Jared gives me a bloody nose or

something. "Nothing is going to happen," I lie.

I *know* that I am telling a lie, because Jared is going to get even for sure. And for no reason, really, except that he is a boy who likes things to get all stirred up. But there's nothing I can do about that. That's just his nature.

Mom is still looking worried. She puts her hand on my sweater, as if her magic touch will keep me from leaving the safety of our red VW. "It's just that Jared is so big, Emma—and you're so tiny. He might hurt you by accident."

I shake away her hand. "You make me sound like an elf or something," I grumble. "I'm not *that* small."

Mom gives me a nervous smile, the kind that doesn't reach her eyes. "Of course you aren't an elf, darling. But a big boy like Jared shouldn't go around hitting a little girl, that's all. A boy shouldn't hit *any* girl. Or even another boy, for that matter."

My mom can be very old-fashioned. As if

a girl wouldn't get in trouble at Oak Glen for slugging a boy—or another girl! This is an equal-opportunity school when it comes to getting in trouble.

"Oh, dear," my mom says, "I think I should go into the school office and talk to someone. I can't just do *nothing*, Em. I'm going to park this stupid car."

"Well, you can't park the car, not here in the loading zone," I tell her. My heart is thunka-thunking underneath my sweater, because I just want her to go home. "You'll get a ticket, and tickets are expensive," I remind her.

"Oh, you're right," she mutters. She peers all around, looking for a regular parking place—which is impossible to find on a Thursday morning when school is just about to start.

"There's Annie Pat waiting for me," I say real fast, before Mom can come up with another terrible plan. "I'll-be-okay-I-love-you-*bye*," I say, and I jump out of the car.

"*Bye,*" I can see my mom's mouth say through the closed window as she gives me a weak little wave.

I try to walk bouncy toward Annie Pat, exactly like a girl who does not know that today is going to be the worst day of her life. Because I'm pretty sure that Mom is still watching me.

But then I hear our car give its little cough and then start up again. She is pulling away from the curb, I think, picturing it.

And I am on my own.

"You should have stayed home," Annie Pat advises me in a tight, worried voice. "You should have changed schools, or moved." We are about to take our seats for roll. Over by the window, Cynthia and Fiona and Heather are taking peeks at me and whispering together. They look worried, as if it is lunchtime already and Jared has just given me two black eyes.

Cynthia is wearing a brand-new pink top, as if this is a special occasion.

Thanks a lot, Cynthia!

"Why should I have stayed home?" I say to Annie Pat, feeling grouchy all of a sudden. "I thought you said I was so brave."

"Well, you *were* brave, yesterday," Annie Pat says. "But," she adds, "I don't think a person ever really knows how brave they're going to be the next time something bad happens. Every single time, it's new. Like when I went to the doctor last week, I had to get a shot, and—and even though everyone was telling me how brave I always am," she says, shivering a little, "all of a sudden, I wasn't brave at all. I just started crying."

Annie Pat can be very scientific about things. And she is so exactly and perfectly right about this one thing that I lose my breath for a second, just as if Jared has already punched me in the stomach.

Because I don't know *how* I'm going to act when Jared tries to make me sorry.

Maybe I'll whine and beg him not to pound me.

Or maybe I'll try to run away from him, with all the kids watching!

Maybe *I'll* be the one to cry—and in front of everyone on the playground, too, just the way Jared wants.

I scowl and plop down into my seat. "Hmmph," I say to Annie Pat. "Gee, thanks a lot."

Annie Pat's big navy blue eyes widen even bigger. "Emma, I didn't mean—"

"Take your seats, boys and girls," Ms. Sanchez

calls out. She waves her engagement-ring hand in the air to get everyone's attention. Our teacher's boyfriend, Mr. Timberlake (like I said before, not the one on MTV), works at a sporting goods store. He is very handsome, even though he's not the famous singer. We saw him once, when he came to school.

Corey Robinson slides into the chair next to me as if he is diving into a swimming pool, which he really does every morning before school. I can tell that he did it this morning, because his hair is all slicked back wet, and I can smell the chlorine.

"Pee-yew," I say. I hold my nose with one hand and wave the air in front of my face with my other hand.

Corey is supposed to grin and say *"Same to you!"* right back, but today he doesn't.

"Jared told me to tell you to go over by the

trash cans in the playground at recess," he whispers instead, as if he is delivering bad news. He gulps and looks over his shoulder.

I take a peek, too.

Yeah, Jared's there, all right. In the back row, the same as always.

Stanley Washington gives Jared a poke in the ribs with his plaid elbow and starts cackling.

Jared waves at me, all fake-friendly and everything.

The whole class is buzzing. It sounds as if there are ten TV sets turned on low in here. "Settle down," Ms. Sanchez says sharply. She is very beautiful, as I said before, but she has X-ray eyes—and she is now zooming them around the room. "I have an important announcement to make," she tells us.

We all sit up straight in our chairs, because maybe it is something about Halloween! We have heard rumors that third-graders usually get to have a party.

Ms. Sanchez starts out slowly. "It has come to my attention . . ." she begins.

Uh-oh. Good announce-ments never start out that way.

"It has come to my

attention that there have been certain threats floating around this classroom," Ms. Sanchez says. "A little bird told me," she adds, as if this is an interesting scientific fact.

Everyone in the whole room—except Ms. Sanchez, of course—tries to look at me as if they are not looking at me.

But it is pretty obvious what they are all thinking: that *I* am the little bird who told.

And I'm not!

It wasn't Mom, either. I'm almost positive about that. And it wasn't Annie Pat, or she would have blabbed about it to me this morning. She could never keep a secret like that.

Kids are whispering. I want to jump up and say, "Hey, it wasn't me," but I can't, for two reasons. Number one, I am stuck to my seat as if someone has poured a big puddle of the world's strongest glue there. Number two, it is against the rules. In our class, you have to raise your hand first, before you jump to your feet and say *anything*.

Well, I guess you would be forgiven if the classroom were on fire, or if you happened to see a highly venomous pit viper slither under someone's desk, but otherwise, no.

Ms. Sanchez is still talking. "Well, I'll have no bullying in this classroom," she snaps. "I don't care what squabbles are going on in here, I'm not going to allow you children to use violence to straighten things out."

Most of us shift back and forth in our seats as if our teacher has just poked us with a fork to see if we're done yet.

We might be done, but she isn't. "Do you have . . . that . . . straight?" she asks us.

"Yeah," we all mumble.

"I want you to say '*Yes, Ms. Sanchez,*'" she instructs us, hands on her hips. "And I want you to mean it."

"Yes, Ms. Sanchez," we finally chant together after a few lame tries.

We say it, and some of us might really mean it.

Me, for instance.

But *living* it is another question, when there are kids like Jared in your class.

x 8 x

Trash

"Where are you going?" Annie Pat squeals. She is tugging urgently at my sweater sleeve. It is morning recess, and I guess Annie Pat is trying to keep me from leaving the classroom.

"I'm going outside," I tell her. "I'm going to stand over by the trash cans. I guess it's time for Jared to teach me a lesson."

"But—but wait, aren't you going to go get your snack first?" Annie Pat asks me, pointing toward the cloakroom, as if I might have forgotten how to get there.

Right. It is obvious that Annie Pat is trying to make time stand still.

"I don't think I'm going to need a snack, not where I'm going," I say gloomily.

I might need Band-Aids, but not a snack.

"*Tweet tweet*," Jared Matthews chirps as he shoves his way past me. By making this noise, he is obviously trying to tell everyone that he thinks I was the little bird who tattled to Ms. Sanchez.

As he walks out the classroom door, Jared looks like an engine that is pulling a train. Behind him, EllRay scowls as he chugs along, and Stanley gives a foolish giggle. Then Stanley gets a bright-idea look in his mean eyes and starts clucking like a chicken—which means that he thinks *I* am chicken. *"Buk buk buk,"* he says.

"Shut up," I tell him.

"Yeah, shut up," someone behind me says. Hey, I think it's Cynthia! Two days ago she admired me, and then yesterday she thought I was stupid. Who knows what she will be thinking tomorrow? It's hard keeping up with her.

"Come *on*, Emma," Annie Pat is begging. "Let's just eat inside."

"For the rest of our lives?" I ask her.

Goldfish lose their orange color if they are kept in dim light.

But I feel almost sorrier for Annie Pat than I do for myself. Her red pigtails, which are usually so springy, seem to be drooping with worry. Her mouth opens and shuts the way a goldfish's mouth does, but like the goldfish, no words come out.

I pull away from Annie Pat's hand and follow the rest of the kids out onto the playground.

Jared is waiting over by the trash cans. He greets me. "Oh, look who's here," he says, rubbing his hands together like a greedy Scrooge McDuck. "It's Super Emma!"

"*I* never called me that," I tell him.

It is strange, but I feel like I am walking in a dream. My steps are bouncy, as though I am stepping on puffy white clouds. And it is as if those same clouds are making every sound a little bit quieter than it usually is, except for the beating of my heart.

"Glad you could make it," Jared says, fake-polite, ignoring my words. But then, I don't think he's even talking to me. He's talking to the circle of kids around him.

I step into the middle of that circle carefully, as if I am getting on an escalator. "Well, I'm here," I say.

"Yeah, after crying like a baby to Ms. Sanchez,"

Jared says. *"Ooo, Teacher, save me, save me,"* he says, pretending to be me.

"I never said that," I tell him—and anybody else who's listening.

"Well, Ms. Sanchez can't save you now," Jared says, laughing. "She's not even here. She's probably drinking coffee." His big square hands are closing into fists, opening, then closing again while he talks. I try not to look at them.

"I don't even want her to save me," I lie. "Just go ahead and sock me, you big bully. Get it over with."

And I get ready to pound him back, even though he probably won't feel a thing—because Jared is *big*. I barely even come up to his chin. Hitting Jared will be like slugging a school bus. Jared will be softer, though. But only a little bit softer.

And I'm going to find out what hitting him feels like pretty soon, because even though I don't have a chance against Jared, I'm not just going to stand here like a big dumb doll.

Around Jared and me, kids have been cramming snacks into their mouths as if they were at the movies or something. But all of a sudden, something changes. It is as though the circle of third-graders is really only one kid, and that kid was a person who started out excited but is now beginning to get mad. "He's going to beat up a *girl*?" someone asks, outraged.

"Look how big he is compared to her," another person calls out, as if this is fast-breaking news. Duh!

"But she asked for it," Stanley cries, defending Jared.

"No she didn't," somebody says. I think it's Annie Pat.

"Yeah," a boy calls out. "It was Jared who stole EllRay's action figure, remember? Emma was just getting it back for EllRay."

Oh, wonderful, I think. *Here we go again about EllRay's action figure.*

Jared is looking around, confused. His hands open and close one more time. Then he speaks.

"Well, I wasn't going to *hit* her," he lies. "I was just going to—to *trash* her."

Nobody knows what this means, exactly, but everyone is eager to find out. It is as though the big circle-person has gone from excited to mad and then back to excited again.

"Do it," Stanley shouts. He picks up an apple core from the ground. "I'll help," he offers. He puts his arm back like he is going to throw the apple core at me, hard.

"You copycat dope," I yell at him. My heart is beating so fast now that I'm kind of surprised it doesn't lift me right off the ground, like a helicopter.

I wish it would!

"No," Jared calls out. "Drop it." As if Stanley was a dog!

Which is not fair to dogs, in my opinion.

The apple core hits the ground.

Jared sneaks peeks all around to make sure everyone is watching him and listening to him. "I'm not going to throw stuff at her," he announces slowly. "I'm going to throw her at *stuff*."

"Huh?" a couple of kids say. They don't know what Jared is talking about.

I don't know either, but I start to get an idea when he lurches forward—and grabs hold of me. "Ow, let me go," I yelp, and we wrestle back and forth for what seems like about a week.

Jared is working his way toward the stinky garbage cans, and he's taking me with him.

He's going to stuff me into a garbage can!

I try to kick his shins, but his arms are wrapped around me so tight that I can't get my feet back far enough to do any good.

My mind fills with jumbled thoughts of what is probably in that trash can.

There will be old tuna fish sandwich scraps.

And mushy bananas.

And yucky, nose-blowing Kleenexes.

Maybe there will even be little plastic bags full of dog poop! I don't know why there would be dog poop in a school trash can, but anything is possible.

I kick at Jared again and hit his leg this time. "*Oof,*" Jared says, and then he crunches me even tighter.

"Dump her," creepy Stanley shouts. "Dump her in the can!"

"I hate you, you big fat meanie," Annie Pat wails.

Poor Annie Pat, I can almost hear myself think. Jared is twisting me over the slimy edge of the fullest garbage can. The smell of the trash fills my head like a tuna-fish-mushy-banana-dog-poop nightmare.

"Let her go," a voice cries out, and another body hurls itself in between Jared and me, knocking the trash can over. Knocking all three of us over!

It's—it's EllRay Jakes!

x 9 x

FOR NO REASON!

I don't know who is the most surprised.

Is it Jared?

Is it me?

Or is it EllRay Jakes?

Jared howls. "You dumb—" and then he starts pounding EllRay's narrow shoulder with his fist. So I pounce on Jared's back like a flea on a bulldog and start whacking *him*.

"Stop . . . it . . . you . . .

big . . . stupid . . . bully," I say, panting. *Thud, thud, thud.* It feels as though I am hitting a mattress.

"I'll bet you're the little bird who tattled to Ms. Sanchez," Jared shouts at EllRay.

"So what if I was?" EllRay shrieks, and he twists around and pops Jared right in the mouth with his fist. I am busy pulling Jared's twirly brown hair, but I have time to be surprised by this news.

EllRay Jakes was the one who tried to keep Jared from teaching me a lesson, even though I was the one who embarrassed EllRay!

"Yow," Jared roars the second after EllRay's fist hits his mouth.

"Two against one, no fair," Stanley squeals, but I don't see *him* jumping into the fight to even things up.

That's Stanley, though.

Suddenly, someone grabs me by the scruff of my neck just as if I were a kitten, and I am lifted off Jared's back. I am being held up in the air by only my sweater and the seat of my pants! I see EllRay go flying up in the air, too, and Jared scrambles to his feet.

"Those two kids were beating Jared up—for no reason," Stanley Washington tells the teacher who is holding me. "It was awful!" he adds, fake-shuddering.

"Shut up, Stanley," Jared cries. His upper lip is already getting puffy. He is starting to look like Daffy Duck, I am happy to see. I sway back and forth in the air like a battering ram, parallel to the ground.

The person holding me—the playground monitor—finally plops me onto my feet. My legs are trembling so much that I can barely stand up. "She pulled out some of Jared's hair," a girl says, sounding amazed.

Sure enough, a few wisps of brown hair are stuck to my hand when I manage to open it. Jared moans and touches the back of his head.

"I'm practically bald!" he says. I wipe my hand on my pants.

"Those two little kids *whomped* him," some kid announces.

"Nuh-uh," Jared shouts, defending his reputation.

EllRay is still dangling in the air like a great big Christmas ornament. "There's not going to be any whomping on *my* playground," the man holding him says, and EllRay sways a little.

I gasp and take a wobbly step back.

It's the principal! The *principal* is holding EllRay Jakes up high in the air.

℀ **10** ℀

a Wish

EllRay and I are in big, big trouble. We are sitting next to each other in the principal's office. This is probably the only time in school history that third-graders have ever been sent to the principal.

Oh, great, we'll be famous—for *this*!

The principal is in the outer office calling our parents. His office door is open, and we can kind of hear what is going on. But EllRay and I just sit here, kicking our feet against the legs of our chairs. EllRay won't even look at me.

I want to say, *"Thank you for trying to save me."*

I want to say, *"I'm really sorry if I embarrassed you the other day."*

Instead, I say, "How is your action figure?"

EllRay gives me an empty look.

"You know," I say helpfully, reminding him. "Your toy. The one with the bat wings, that Jared took." But now I am starting to wish that I had kept my big mouth shut.

"Oh. It's fine," EllRay says. He tries to smile, but then he goes back to kicking the chair.

Jared is in the nurse's office, even though he kept telling everyone that he was okay. But the nurse just walked by holding a bowl of ice from the cafeteria. I guess it's for Jared's swollen mouth. Our school nurse looks just like a regular lady. She doesn't wear a uniform, or anything like that, but she does peek into the principal's office as she passes.

I guess she wants to see the rough, tough kids who were mean enough to hit poor Jared Matthews.

Hah.

"All right," the principal says, bustling into his office. "I've talked with both your parents." He towers above us, looking down, hands on his hips. I sneak a peek at his face. He has a very large nose and a black beard. It is so fluffy that

I'm surprised words can get past his hidden lips. "Emma?" he says, turning to me.

"Yes?" I croak.

"Your mother told me some of what's been happening. Jared's threat and so on. You should have spoken to Ms. Sanchez about it, Miss."

Miss. I'm really in trouble now. Or maybe he just can't remember my last name.

"Okay," I say meekly. But I know that I would probably still be sitting here, in trouble, even if I *did* tell on Jared. Because Jared wanted a fight.

"And you, young fella," the principal says, turning to EllRay, "you and your pop did the right thing by calling the school office this morning."

EllRay ducks his head and blushes, waiting for what is going to come next.

And here it comes. "But there's absolutely no excuse for fighting," the principal states.

"I didn't mean to fight," EllRay says. "But see, Jared was going to—"

"There's no excuse, *period*," the principal interrupts—which is very rude, I think. But it is his office, so I keep my mouth shut.

"Yes sir," EllRay mumbles.

"Now, your parents and I have talked it over, and I decided that I'm going to let you kids return to class today. All three of you," the principal says, jerking his head toward the nurse's office, next door, where Jared is. "But I don't want any more trouble, do you hear me?"

EllRay and I nod. How could we not hear him? His voice is booming all over the place. Even Jared can probably hear him!

"Because if there *is* any more trouble, especially any more hitting," he says, bending over to stare us in the eyes, "I'm going to be very, very upset, understand? And you don't want that to happen. Believe me."

"*I believe you*," EllRay and I both say at the exact same time.

"All right, you two can go now," the principal

says. Jared will rejoin your class in half an hour or so, when the swelling goes down."

And so EllRay and I trudge back to class down the long, shiny, empty hallway.

EllRay turns to me. "I wasn't being brave when I tried to defend you," he says to me. "I just couldn't figure out what else to do."

"I know exactly what you mean," I tell him.

χ χ χ

Phew. We are finally eating lunch after a long morning of listening to Ms. Sanchez be mad at us about what happened at recess. We had to raise our hands one at a time and tell her ways to solve problems when you are angry, ways that don't have hitting in them.

I don't think that any of the things we came up with would work with a kid like Jared Matthews, but I guess making that list helped Ms. Sanchez calm down a little.

Some of the answers kids had were pretty good. For instance, Fiona said you could draw an ugly picture of the kid you are mad at and then crumple it up. That sounded like fun.

But some of the ideas were dumb. For example, Heather suggested that you should say, *"I am just so angry at you!"* to the person you're mad at. And what good would that do? If you said that to someone like Jared, he would be absolutely thrilled!

But Ms. Sanchez wrote it down on the board anyway.

"Are you okay?" Cynthia asks me as I am peeking into my lunch sack.

"I'm fine," I tell her. Annie Pat and I are eating with the other third-grade girls again, so everything is back to normal.

Or *almost* normal, because the whole playground is buzzing with news about the big fight. Kindergartners, first-graders, and second-graders are looking at EllRay and me as if we are the king and queen of Oak Glen Primary School. They have been bullied by Jared for so long—for years!—that EllRay and I are now their champions.

But we are trying to be modest about the whole thing. Because that's the best way for heroes to be.

Heather offers me some of her cheese and crackers. "I was so scared during the fight," she says, pulling her jacket close around her.

"*Me, too,*" I feel like saying, but I don't.

People don't like their champions to be fraidy-cats.

Annie Pat nibbles at a corner of her sandwich, then says, "But Emma, do you think Jared is going to try to get you again? He still looks so mad!"

"He looks so *silly,*" Fiona corrects her, "with his lip all puffed up and everything."

The girls all gaze at me admiringly for a moment, even though it was EllRay who socked Jared in the mouth. I just pulled out some of his hair.

"Jared's not going to be starting any more fights," Cynthia says, sounding wise.

"How can you be so sure?" Annie Pat wants to know.

"Because he knows that the whole entire class will hate him if we have to spend another morning making ways-to-solve-problems lists on the board," Cynthia says smugly.

Good point. Sometimes, in spite of everything, Cynthia can be pretty smart.

X X X

It is bedtime now, and Mom smoothes the hair back from my forehead and tucks the quilt up under my chin. "I love you, Emma," she says into the darkness.

"Me, too," I say.

She knows what I mean.

"Well . . ." she says, and she starts to stand up.

"Mom?" I ask quickly. "Is anybody *really* brave?"

Mom settles back down. "What do you mean, honey?" she asks.

I think for a second. "The first time kids thought I was brave, it was only because I got mad," I say. "And the second time I acted brave, I was really just scared. And the third time kids thought I was brave, which was today, I was only trying to keep from getting trashed."

Mom leans over and gives me a squeeze when she hears these last words.

"It's kind of like what EllRay told me this morning, after he hit Jared," I murmur. "He said he just couldn't figure out what else to do. That's the way *I* feel. But is that the same thing as being brave?"

"Well," Mom says, "you already know that *I* think you're brave, honey. And as for EllRay, what were all the other kids doing when Jared was dragging you toward the trash can?"

"Watching," I tell her, picturing the circle of excited faces.

"Then I think that what EllRay did took a lot

of courage," Mom says. "Watching bullies and standing up to them are two separate things, Em."

I shut my eyes and whisper a secret to my mom. "I don't want to fight anymore. I just want there to be peace and quiet."

Mom laughs. "Well, Super Emma," she says, "I don't know about anyplace else in the world, but there's peace and quiet for you here at home."

"I know," I say, smiling in the dark.

X X X

I can hear my mom brushing her teeth.

I listen to a car drive by, and a block away, a dog barks. Another dog answers him.

They do that.

Behind a golden seashell, my night-light is glowing. If I shut my eyes halfway, it looks almost like a star.

We *are* going to have a Halloween party, Ms. Sanchez told us this afternoon! But only if we can be good, and work on solving our problems in a reasonable, civilized way.

I'm pretty sure that we can. Because we *like* parties!

I close my eyes and make a wish.